GRUMPY BUNNY TALES

by Justine Korman Fontes
Illustrated by Lucinda McQueen

SCHOLASTIC INC.

New York Toronto London Auckland
Sydney Mexico City New Delhi Hong Kong

ISBN 978-0-545-22943-2

Clean Up, Grumpy Bunny!
ISBN 978-0-439-68779-9
Text copyright © 2006 by Justine Korman Fontes.
Illustrations copyright © 2006 by Lucinda McQueen.

Tell the Truth, Grumpy Bunny!
ISBN 978-0-439-02011-4
Text copyright © 2008 by Justine Korman Fontes.
Illustrations copyright © 2008 by Lucinda McQueen.

Wait Your Turn, Grumpy Bunny!
ISBN 978-0-439-68781-2
Text copyright © 2007 by Justine Korman Fontes.
Illustrations copyright © 2007 by Lucinda McQueen.

Please Say Please, Grumpy Bunny!
ISBN 978-0-439-02012-1
Text copyright © 2007 by Justine Korman Fontes.
Illustrations copyright © 2007 by Lucinda McQueen.

Time Out, Grumpy Bunny!
ISBN 978-0-439-68780-5
Text copyright © 2005 by Justine Korman Fontes.
Illustrations copyright © 2005 by Lucinda McQueen.

Let's Share, Grumpy Bunny!
ISBN 978-0-439-68782-9
Text copyright © 2006 by Justine Korman Fontes.
Illustrations copyright © 2006 by Lucinda McQueen.

12 11 10 9 8 7 6 5 4 3 2 1   10 11 12 13 14 15/0

Printed in the U.S.A.   40

First Scholastic printing, January 2010

CLEAN UP, GRUMPY BUNNY!

by Justine Korman Fontes

Illustrated by Lucinda McQueen

For Candace Miller Rice,
inventor of the Millerian Principals of Neatness
—J.K.F.

For little Miss Molly
—Love, Lucy

Chapter 1
Mr. Mess

Hopper O'Hare was messy.

He took out many toys during playtime.
But Hopper never put any away.

Playtime was over.
"Clean up!" said Mrs. Clover.
But Hopper did not.

"Aren't you going to help?"
asked Corny.
"I'm busy reading!" Hopper said.
"You're always busy during cleanup,"
Corny said.
But Hopper just went back to reading
his book.

"It isn't fair!" Marigold cried.
"Hopper makes the biggest mess.
But he never cleans up."
"Why should we clean up
Hopper's mess?" Corny said.
"You're right," Mrs. Clover said.
"Hopper should clean up, too."

"You will miss hippety-hop practice
if you don't start cleaning up,"
Mrs. Clover said.

Hopper didn't listen.
No one ever missed hippety-hop!
Hippety-hop was even more important
than painting eggs or making baskets.

Chapter 2
Clean Up...or Else!

Mrs. Clover told the other bunnies
not to clean up for Hopper.

"Please begin your hippety-hops
while Hopper cleans up," she said.

"Me? Clean up? All alone?"
Hopper asked.
"Yes," Mrs. Clover said.
"You'll have to miss hippety-hop
until you learn to clean up."
"Oh, worms!" Hopper cried.
"I hate cleaning up!"

Mrs. Clover patted his shoulder.
"Cleaning up after yourself is
part of growing up," she said.
"Wiggly worms on toast,"
Hopper said.

Then Lilac Lapin raised her paw.
"May I help Hopper? I like cleaning up."
Mrs. Clover agreed.

Hopper couldn't believe his ears.
"How can anyone like cleaning up?"
"Cleaning up is a game," Lilac explained.

Chapter 3
The Game

"I pretend I'm a librarian when I put away books," she said.

"Being a librarian would be fun,"
Hopper said. "Then I could read
all the books I want."
Soon Hopper and Lilac had put away
all the books.

"I like to put away cars," Lilac said.
"I pretend I run a parking garage."

Hopper handed Lilac a truck.
"Beep! Beep! Make room for a big one,"
he said.
Soon all the toy trucks and cars were
neatly parked.

"Now let's put all the friends together," Lilac said.
"Friends?" Hopper asked.
Lilac giggled. "I pretend things that are alike are friends. Blocks belong with blocks, robots with robots..."

"I get it!" Hopper shouted.
"Friends are happier when they're together," Lilac said. "So cleaning up is a happy thing."

Hopper put a T. rex on the shelf with the
other dinosaurs.
"Now you won't be lonely," he told the toy.
Hopper giggled.
Lilac laughed, too.

Then, they rounded up the toy horses.
Hopper smiled. "I hope they'll be happy
at the Big Shelf Ranch."

"I like to put little things in front
of big things," Lilac said.
"That way the little ones won't
miss the view."

She tucked a little teddy bear
on the shelf.
"Now he can see everything,"
Hopper said.

Chapter 4
Chore No More

"Cleaning up helps me find my toys," Lilac said.

Hopper held up a block.
"I have never seen this one before,"
he said. "It would make a cool cave
next time we play with blocks."

Hopper was almost sad when
they were done.

Then, he laughed.
"What's so funny?" Lilac asked.
"I can't wait to go home and clean up
my room!" Hopper said.

Mrs. Clover thanked Hopper and Lilac
for doing a good job.
"I hope you'll clean up after yourself
from now on," she told Hopper.
"Cleaning up is way too much fun to skip!"
Hopper said.

TELL THE TRUTH, GRUMPY BUNNY!

To Roy Wandelmaier and everybunny else
who struggles to stay solid in a hollow world.
—J.K.F.

In memory of our sweet brother and sister, Vincie and Alice.
—Lucy

TELL THE TRUTH, GRUMPY BUNNY!

by Justine Korman Fontes
Illustrated by Lucinda McQueen

Chapter 1
Little Bunny, Big Mouth

Hopper sometimes stretched the truth
to make his stories more exciting.
He told his friends, "I caught a fish as
big as our boat!"
"Where's the fish?" Corny asked.
"We had to throw it back—or sink,"
Hopper said.
"Wow!" Corny exclaimed.
And Hopper smiled.
He liked when his friends said "Wow!"

One day, everybunny was talking
about chocolate.
"My family always buys Solid-Chocolate
Bunnies," Hopper said.
Corny didn't quite hear. "Did you say
your family knows The Solid-Chocolate
Bunny?"

Hopper couldn't help himself.
He began another story. "Dad worked
with him in the city," he said.

Suddenly everybunny was listening
and asking questions.
"What's he like?"
"What's his real name?"
"Is he really tall, dark, and honest?"

Hopper loved all the attention.
And his lie seemed harmless.
Until…

...Sir Byron, the principal, said, "Then
Hopper must already know my surprise."
Hopper's ears tingled.
"The Solid-Chocolate Bunny himself will be
at school tomorrow," Sir Byron said.

Everybunny cheered!
But Hopper's stomach sank.
Tomorrow everybunny would find out that
his story wasn't true!

Chapter 2
A Very Dark Night

Hopper didn't know what to do.
Should he pretend to be sick and stay
home from school?

Then Hopper heard Marigold talking to
Lilac. "Do you think Hopper really knows
The Solid-Chocolate Bunny?"
Lilac giggled. "Can he catch a fish as big
as a boat?"

That night, Hopper couldn't fall asleep.
So he made a wish on a star.
Hopper wished that he could stop
telling lies.
He wished that his friends would still
like him.
And that somehow everything would
work out.

Finally, Hopper fell asleep.
But his dreams were all a jumble.
In one, Hopper was being chased by
an army of angry chocolate bunnies!

In another, Hopper was caught by a
giant fish!
"Let me go! Let me go!" Hopper cried.
But the fish just laughed.

The next morning, Hopper was very tired
and very grumpy.
He could barely brush his teeth.
Hopper dragged his feet to the bus stop.
He was just in time—to miss the bus!
"Oh, worms!" Hopper cried. "Now I'll
have to walk to school."

Chapter 3
Fast Friends

Soon Hopper saw someone on the
path ahead.
The someone was tall and dark.
Could it be?
Hopper ran ahead to see.
It was.
"The Solid-Chocolate Bunny!"
Hopper cried.

"In the fur," the big bunny replied.
"Actually, my name is Felix Moss."
He shook Hopper's paw. "I hope we
can be friends."
Hopper's paw felt lost in warm fur.
*I hope it happens before we get to
school*, he thought.

Just as Hopper hoped, the two became
friends.
The Solid-Chocolate Bunny tested his
speech on Hopper.

"When I was young, I bit a hollow, fake-chocolate bunny. Did I like it?" Hopper shook his head. "No, sir!"

Before long, their sunny walk was over.
Sir Byron himself came out to greet them.
"Welcome!" he said.

Then he saw Hopper and added,
"Why don't we let your old friend
Hopper introduce you?"
Hopper could hardly believe his good luck.
His story was turning true!
If only Mr. Moss would go along with it.

Chapter 4
One Last Lie

"That would be grand!" Felix agreed.
Hopper whispered, "Please don't tell
anyone we just met."
It was time to go on.

Hopper said, "I'd like you all to meet
my good friend, Felix Moss, also known
as The Solid-Chocolate Bunny."
Everybunny cheered, "Hooray!"

Hopper felt happy—until the end of
Mr. Moss's speech.
Felix thanked Sir Byron and his new
friend Hopper O'Hare.
"Even though we only met this morning,
I'm sure we'll be great friends,"
The Solid-Chocolate Bunny said.

Everybunny burst out laughing.
Hopper blushed red and he felt
like crying.

Hopper felt someone's paw tap his
shoulder.
Lilac whispered, "Don't cry."
Then Corny clapped Hopper on the back.
"Tell us how you really met Mr. Moss."
Hopper smiled. "Well, I missed the bus
this morning and…"
"…took the same flying saucer as The
Solid-Chocolate Bunny?" Marigold teased.

Lilac laughed. "It's okay, Hopper. We like your silly stories."

"Yeah," Corny agreed. "But we like to hear the truth, too."

So Hopper told the story exactly as it happened.

And Corny said, "Wow!" anyway.

Later, Mr. Moss said, "Hopper, you're too nice a bunny to fall into bad habits. Tell the truth and everybunny will love you. I promise."
Of course, Hopper believed him.
He felt solid and warm inside.
Hopper told the truth from that day on.

WAIT YOUR TURN, GRUMPY BUNNY!

For Granny Valerie and everybunny else whose patience makes
the world a nicer place.
—J.K.F.

For Katherine and Jim...and "MainStreet BookEnds"!
—Lots of Love, Lucinda

WAIT YOUR TURN, GRUMPY BUNNY!

by Justine Korman Fontes
Illustrated by Lucinda McQueen

Chapter 1
Hurry Up and Wait

Hopper O'Hare hurried to the bus stop.
"Worms!" he said. "School days are just
one long line."
He waited on line to get on the bus.
Then he waited on line to get off the bus.

Hopper had to wait to get a drink of water.

He had to wait to use a scooter in gym class.

Hopper even had to wait during
arts and crafts time.
"Lilac is using the purple crayon
now," Mrs. Violet told Hopper.
"You'll have to wait."
Hopper's ears turned red.
He was sick of waiting!

Hopper had a question during story time.
He raised his paw and waited.
Hopper waited a long time.
He forgot his question!
Everyone laughed.

Chapter 2
King Hopper

Finally, it was time for recess!
Hopper couldn't wait to have some fun.
But there was a line for the swings.
"Wiggly worms!" Hopper said. "I wish
I lived somewhere without any lines."

If I were king of my own country . . .
Hopper began to daydream.
Kings never wait on line,
he thought. *Wouldn't that be great?*

Hopper thought about being first
at the water fountain,

first at the library,

and first at lunch.

It was always Hopper's turn in Hopperland!

There was no waiting—ever!

There was no waiting at the movies.

There were no lines at the skating rink.

Chapter 3
King of the Swings

But soon, there was nobody to play with!
All of King Hopper's friends went away.
No one wanted to play with him.
Swings are no fun alone, Hopper thought.
*Even a king needs someone to give him
a push.*

The seesaw was even worse than the swings. Hopper sighed. "Toys are no fun without friends."

Hopper decided he didn't want to
be king any more.
"I'd rather wait my turn than play
alone," he said.

Chapter 4
Next!

Just then, Hopper heard Coach Parsley
shout, "Next!"

Hopper's best friend, Corny Cabbage, cried,
"Take your turn!"

"Carrots and jellybeans!" Hopper said.
"It's finally my turn!"

Hopper jumped onto the swing.
Corny started pushing.
"Higher!" Hopper squeaked. "Whee!"
Hopper swung so high he got dizzy.
And he didn't mind when his turn was over.

Hopper went to Corny's house after school.
Corny had so many brothers and sisters.
There was a line for everything!
But Hopper didn't mind.
He was glad to wait his turn.

Everyone cheered when Hopper
made a basket.
Hopper knew that having friends
was even better than being king.

PLEASE SAY PLEASE, GRUMPY BUNNY!

PLEASE SAY PLEASE, GRUMPY BUNNY!

by Justine Korman Fontes
Illustrated by Lucinda McQueen

Chapter 1
The Magic Word

One morning, Mrs. Clover asked her class,
"Does anyone know the magic word?"
Hopper O'Hare's ears flew up.
A magic word!
Would it bring toys to life?
Or make bunnies fly?

No one could guess.
"The magic word is *please*,"
Mrs. Clover said.
Hopper's ears drooped.
He rolled his eyes.
The word *please* wasn't magical.
It was just one of those polite words
grown-ups fussed about,
like *thank you* and *excuse me*.

Hopper wasn't used to
saying please.
He was an only-bunny.
Hopper never had to ask brothers
or sisters for things.
And at Corny's crowded house,
everybunny was too busy playing
to bother with saying please.

Chapter 2
The Game

"We are going to play a Please Day game," Mrs. Clover said. "The winner will be any bunny who says please perfectly all day long.

That means saying please every time you ask for anything."

Hopper decided to win the Please Day game.

This should be easy, he thought.

But remembering to say please every time
you ask for something isn't easy.
Mrs. Clover's class played basketball
during gym.
It was a very exciting game!
Marigold got near the basket.
She shouted, "Pass the ball to me!"

Everybunny froze.

Corny stopped dribbling.
Suddenly, Marigold realized her mistake.
"Oh, no, I forgot to say please!"

Hopper felt sorry for Marigold.
He was determined not to make the
same mistake.

Chapter 3
The Surprise Bonus

"May I please write on the blackboard?"
Hopper asked later.
Hopper loved to write on the board.
Mrs. Clover smiled. She let him write all
the math problems.

In the cafeteria, Snowball asked, "May
I have the big brownie?"
"You forgot the magic word!" Corny
exclaimed.
Hopper added, "You should have said,
'May I *please* have the big brownie?'"
The cafeteria bunny smiled.
Then she gave Hopper the big brownie.
Hopper was beginning to like saying please!

At the library, Mrs. Pumpkin asked,
"Who wants to read this book?"
Milkweed's paw flew up. "May I?" he asked.
"Aren't you forgetting something?"
Mrs. Pumpkin asked.
Hopper raised his paw. "May I please have
the book?"
Mrs. Pumpkin smiled. "That's very
polite, Hopper."

Hopper let Milkweed have the book.
But Milkweed was out of the Please Day game.

In music class, Hopper struggled with
his scales.
"Let me show you," Lilac said.
Hopper's ears flew up. She'd forgotten
the magic word!

Lilac blushed. "Oops! I should have said please."
Now even polite Lilac was out of the game.

Hopper kept saying please all day long.

And the strangest thing happened.

He started to think the word might really *be* magic!

Chapter 4
The Winner!

"May I please have your attention?"
Mrs. Clover asked at the end of the day.
"Who remembered to say please all day?
If you did, please raise your paw now."
Hopper's paw flew up.
He looked around the room. He was the
only one!
Mrs. Clover smiled. "We have a winner."

Hopper felt very proud and happy.
He had won the game!
But Hopper kept saying please.

Corny wondered why Hopper was still saying please.

Hopper shrugged. "I like the way please makes everybunny smile."

"I noticed that, too," Corny said.

"But why?" Corny wondered.

Hopper said, "Nobunny likes to do what they're told. But they're happy to do what they're asked."

"That makes sense," Corny agreed.

"Besides," Hopper added. "I want to win the next Please Day game, too. I might as well practice."

Corny laughed.

"May I please come over to your house
after school?" he asked Hopper.

Maybe *he* would win the next game.

Then they both burst out laughing.

TIME OUT, GRUMPY BUNNY!

For all the librarians who shush and share.
—J.K.F.

For Tucker.
—Love, Lucy

TIME OUT, GRUMPY BUNNY!

by Justine Korman Fontes
Illustrated by Lucinda McQueen

Chapter 1
A Bad Morning

"Oh, worms! I'm late!"
cried Hopper O'Hare.

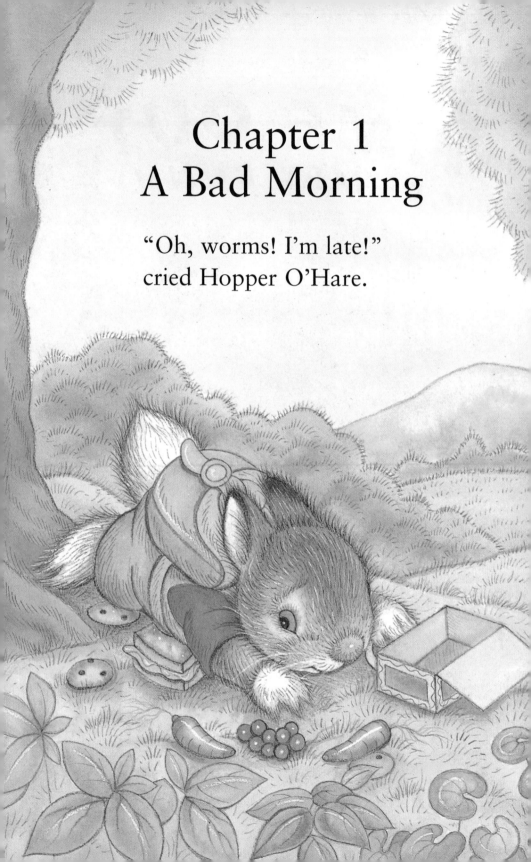

He ran toward school.
SMACK!
Hopper fell on his lunch!

Hopper put his mushy lunch
into his cubby.
He saw Corny, Lilac, and Marigold
put away their library books.

"Oh, more wiggly worms!" Hopper said.
"I forgot my books!"
His ears turned red.

"It's time for math,"
Mrs. Clover said.
She wrote the homework problems
on the board.

Hopper's ears turned even redder.
"I did the wrong pages!" he cried.
Mrs. Clover said, "*Shh!*"

Then she added, "Hopper, please do the first one."
Hopper was still mad about doing the wrong pages.
So he made a mistake.

Mrs. Clover fixed Hopper's answer.
"Oh, wiggly worms on toast!"
Hopper said. "I knew that!"

But it was too late.

Chapter 2
At the Library

Hopper looked out the window.
His ears fell.
"Mushy lunch and rain clouds,"
Hopper said. "This day is just
one long worm."

"At least it's Library Day,"
said Lilac Lapin.
Hopper smiled.
He loved Library Day.

Soon, Hopper's class lined up
in front of the library.
"Oh, crunchy carrots!" Hopper cried.
"New books!"

Mrs. Pumpkin greeted the class
at the door.
The librarian held her finger
to her lips.
She said, "*Shh!*"

Hopper found a great book.
"Hey, Corny!" he said.

Hopper forgot to whisper.

Suddenly, there was a loud *Shh!*
Mrs. Pumpkin was right behind them!

Hopper almost jumped out of his fur.

Later, Hopper and Corny waited
in line to check out books.
"Oh, worms!" Hopper said.
"This is taking too long!"
Marigold turned around.
She said, "*Shh!*"

Finally, it was Hopper's turn.
"You can't check those out yet,"
Mrs. Pumpkin said.
"You need to bring back
the old books first."

Hopper's ears turned bright red.
His face felt hot.
Every rotten thing that had happened
flashed before his eyes.

Suddenly, Hopper threw down the books.
THUMP!
Everyone in the library stared at Hopper.
Mrs. Pumpkin frowned.
"Hopper O'Hare, you need a time out,"
she said. "Please go to Sir Byron's office."

Chapter 3
The Rain Storm

Hopper's heart thumped.
He walked down the long hall all alone.

Hopper had never been
to the principal's office!
Would Sir Byron yell at him?
Would he call his mother?
Would Hopper have to stay after school?

Hopper sat down in Sir Byron's office.
"Everyone gets angry sometimes,"
Sir Byron said. "When we get angry,
it feels like a storm inside us.
The sky gets dark.
Thunder BOOMS and lightning CRASHES.
And the rain pours down."
"I felt like that in the library!"
Hopper said.
Sir Byron smiled.

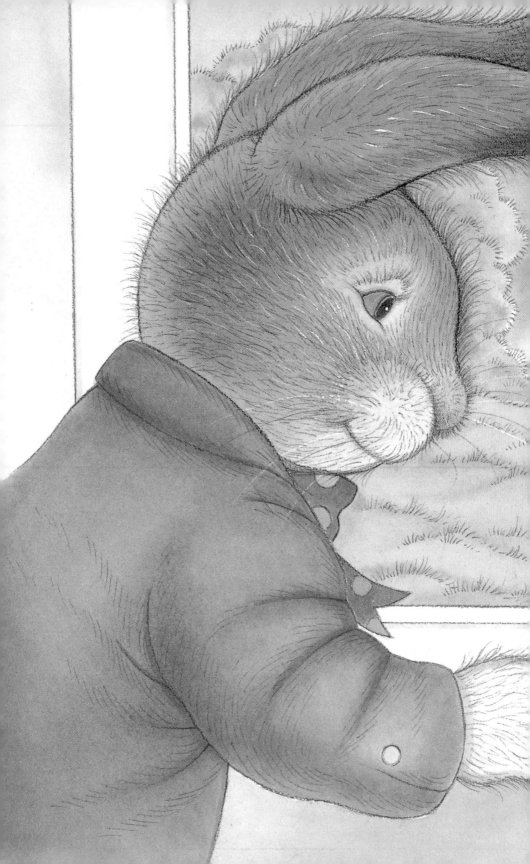

"But when the storm ends,
there is a rainbow," Sir Byron said.
Hopper looked out the window.
The clouds were gone.
The storm was over.
"Look!" Hopper said.
"There's a rainbow!"

Chapter 4
A Happy Bunny

"Are you ready to go back to class?"
Sir Byron asked.
Hopper nodded.
He felt as calm as the sky.

He felt a lot better.
He knew other storms would come.
But he also knew they would pass.

The next day, Hopper brought
his library books to school.
"I'm sorry I lost my temper yesterday,"
he told Mrs. Pumpkin.
The librarian smiled.
"Everyone gets angry sometimes,"
she said.

Then she took out a stack of books.
"I saved these for you," she said.
His books!
Hopper smiled.

Hopper thanked Mrs. Pumpkin.
Then he hopped down the hall
back to class.

LET'S SHARE, GRUMPY BUNNY!

LET'S SHARE, GRUMPY BUNNY!

by Justine Korman Fontes
Illustrated by Lucinda McQueen

Chapter 1
Seeing Red

Hopper O'Hare loved art class.
But he didn't like sharing paints.
Everyone always wanted to use the
same color.

Hopper reached for the blue paint.
So did Lilac.
The cup spilled!
"Worms!" Hopper said.
"I'm sorry," Lilac said.

Everyone always forgot to wash
the brushes.
"You got red in the yellow!" Hopper
yelled at Marigold.
"I'm sorry," Marigold said.

The art teacher talked to Hopper.
"You are a very good artist," Mrs.
Violet said. "But you have to learn
to share."
Hopper sighed. "Wiggly worms!"
he said.

"Would you like to paint a poster?"
Mrs. Violet asked Hopper.

Hopper's ears flew up.
He clapped his paws.

"You will work with Corny,"
Mrs. Violet added.
Hopper's ears flopped down.
"But, I…"
"This is your chance to share,"
Mrs. Violet said.
Hopper grumbled.

Chapter 2
Hey, You, Get Out
of My Blue!

Hopper wanted to paint the poster.
So he had to share.
The boys decided to paint a big
meadow.

But they kept bumping in to each other.
Hopper tried moving.
Corny's elbows were everywhere!

Corny painted the tree trunk.
"That's my tree!" Hopper said.
Corny splashed brown paint on
Hopper's nose.
"Sorry," he said.

Hopper painted green grass.
"That looks like fun!" Corny said.
Corny painted green grass, too.
"I think I'll add some red and blue
flowers," he said.

He dipped his brush into the cup.
Uh-oh!

Chapter 3
Purple Power

Corny forgot to wash his brush.
The sky had a red swirl in it!
Hopper was so angry!
His ears turned as red as the paint.
"Wiggly worms on toast!" Hopper yelled.
"You got red paint in the blue!"
"I'm sorry," Corny said.

Hopper looked at the poster.
Getting angry won't help, he thought.
Hopper calmed down by counting to ten.
Just then, Hopper saw a purple swirl.
He had an idea!

Hopper took an empty paint cup.
He poured in a little red and a little blue.
He mixed them until he had purple.
"Let's add a purple monster to our
meadow!" Hopper said.
"That's a great idea!" Corny said.
"The Great Grape Googly-Moogly!"
Hopper shouted.

The boys painted a big, purple monster.
It was fun!

Chapter 4
The Great Grape
Googly-Moogly

Hopper and Corny kept painting.
They did not fight.
"I'm so glad we added the monster,"
Corny said. "The meadow was boring
without him."

Mrs. Violet came over to check
their work.

"He's a wonderful monster," she said.
"The Great Grape Googly-Moogly!"
the boys shouted together.

Mrs. Violet hung up the poster.
"I'm very proud of you, Hopper,"
Mrs. Violet said.

"You calmed down and solved
your problem. You both painted
a great poster. And you did it by
sharing."

Hopper felt very proud and happy.
Now he would share everything.
Sharing was a lot of fun!